WELCOME TO
PASSPORT TO READING
A beginning reader's ticket to a brand-new world!

Every book in this program is designed to build read-along and read-alone skills, level by level, through engaging and enriching stories. As the reader turns each page, he or she will become more confident with new vocabulary, sight words, and comprehension.

These PASSPORT TO READING levels will help you choose the perfect book for every reader.

READING TOGETHER
Read short words in simple sentence structures together to begin a reader's journey.

READING OUT LOUD
Encourage developing readers to sound out words in more complex stories with simple vocabulary.

READING INDEPENDENTLY
Newly independent readers gain confidence reading more complex sentences with higher word counts.

READY TO READ MORE
Readers prepare for chapter books with fewer illustrations and longer paragraphs.

This book features sight words from the educator-supported Dolch Sight Words List. This encourages the reader to recognize commonly used vocabulary words, increasing reading speed and fluency.

For more information, please visit passporttoreadingbooks.com.

Enjoy the journey!

Little, Brown and Company

Hachette Book Group
1290 Avenue of the Americas, New York, NY 10104
Visit us at lb-kids.com

Little, Brown and Company is a division of Hachette Book Group, Inc.
The Little, Brown name and logo are trademarks of Hachette Book Group, Inc.

The publisher is not responsible for websites (or their content)
that are not owned by the publisher.

First Edition: January 2015

Library of Congress Control Number: 2013957724

ISBN 978-0-316-40558-4

10 9 8 7 6 5 4 3

CW

PRINTED IN THE UNITED STATES OF AMERICA

Passport to Reading titles are leveled by independent reviewers applying the standards developed by Irene Fountas and Gay Su Pinnell in *Matching Books to Readers: Using Leveled Books in Guided Reading*, Heinemann, 1999.

Licensed By:

Meet Optimus Primal

Adapted by **Jennifer Fox**

Based on the episode "Big Game"
written by **Greg Johnson**

LITTLE, BROWN AND COMPANY
New York   Boston

Attention, Rescue Bots fans!
Look for these words when you read
this book. Can you spot them all?

truck

hunter

blaster

frozen

Optimus Prime is the brave
leader of the Rescue Bots.

Boulder, Chase,
Heatwave, and Blades
are on his team.

Optimus Prime can change
from a robot...

...into a powerful truck
that can even travel underwater!

He can also change into…

...Optimus Primal!

This is his dino mode.

He is a T. rex.

In dino form, Optimus Primal
takes his friend Cody
for a wild ride.

"Hold on!" Optimus shouts.
He races across the grass.

Optimus Primal roars!

His roar shakes the trees.

A greedy hunter named
Colonel Quarry sees Optimus Primal
in the forest.

"A dino bot!" the hunter shouts.

Colonel Quarry chases Optimus.

He wants to catch him.

Optimus has another idea.

He chases the hunter!

The hunter reaches
for his blaster.

Optimus stomps on it
with one mighty foot.

The hunter set a trap.

Icy mist covers

Optimus and Cody.

Optimus Primal is frozen!

"It is c-c-cold!" says Cody.

Boulder rushes to the rescue.

"I have your back!"
the Rescue Bot calls.
Boulder brings the hunter's Heli-jet
to the ground.

Boulder changes into dino mode.

He is now a triceratops.

The hunter is getting away!
Optimus and Boulder charge
to stop him for good.

They catch the hunter!

Optimus brings his pal Cody
back home.

Optimus Prime is a strong leader
and protects humans.

He is even stronger with a great team
like the Rescue Bots!

Optimus Prime
and the Rescue Bots
are always there
for one another!